Joey and His Friend Water

Ellen J Lewinberg

Joey and His Friend Water
Copyright © 2023 by Ellen J Lewinberg

All rights reserved. No part of this publication may be reproduced, distributed, or transmitted in any form or by any means, including photocopying, recording, or other electronic or mechanical methods, without the prior written permission of the author, except in the case of brief quotations embodied in critical reviews and certain other non-commercial uses permitted by copyright law.

Tellwell Talent
www.tellwell.ca

ISBN
978-0-2288-8169-8 (Paperback)
978-0-2288-9559-6 (eBook)

To my grandchildren, Eli, Isaac and Martin, and to children and their parents everywhere.

Table of Contents

Chapter 1 A Voice in the Forest 1

Chapter 2 In Trouble Again 11

Chapter 3 What to Think 15

Chapter 4 Back in the Forest 19

Chapter 5 Checking the Facts 24

Chapter 6 Back to the Stream 29

Chapter 7 More Voices in the Forest 37

Chapter 8 The Role of Trees 39

Chapter 9 Someone to Talk To 48

Chapter 10 Joey Visits Alice 50

Chapter 11 Back to the Stream 57

Chapter 12 Saving the Forest 62

Chapter 13 Alice Meets Water 66

Chapter 14 Everything is Energy 74

Chapter 15 Nature Spirits in the Garden 81

About the Author 86

Acknowledgements 87

References 88

Chapter 1
A Voice in the Forest

Joey lived in a house that looked rather ordinary, but there was something special about the backyard. Behind the house was a forest. And, in that forest was a stream that twisted and turned. It also had a little waterfall and a pond big enough to swim in.

Joey loved playing in the forest with his friends. They played all sorts of games, like hide and seek and enchanted forest. Everyone knows how to play hide and seek, but maybe not how to play enchanted forest. In this game they would pretend to be either a wizard or witch, casting spells and making concoctions with leaves, sticks, or anything else they could find. It was so much fun! But best of all was when they got hot from running around, they would jump into the pond to cool off. Of course, they had to find an adult to supervise before they could go swimming. Safety first!

Joey's parents had told him not to go into the woods by himself. They thought he was too young and might get hurt falling out of a tree. He loved climbing trees. Sitting high up in a tree, he felt like he could see for miles and was at the top of the world. But he really liked being in the forest by himself because it was so quiet and peaceful. The only noises he heard were the stream rushing over the rocks, the trees sighing in the wind, the birds singing, and the little animals rushing about doing whatever it was that they did. Joey would sometimes sneak out to sit by the stream, especially if he was in trouble or when he just wanted to be by himself and think.

The moss that grew near the stream was so soft to lie on. It was friendly and inviting. And Joey loved the sound of the water flowing in the stream. He liked to listen to the water gurgle over the stones and the loud splash of the waterfall. He enjoyed lying on his back and looking up at the sky through the leaves on the trees. It was so nice to lie in the cool shade on a hot summer's day listening to the bees buzzing and the birds singing. It was beautiful.

Joey was lying by the stream one afternoon after a hard day. He had been in trouble at school because he had left his homework at home. He had done the work, but his teacher didn't believe that he had completed it. Joey was still a bit upset with his teacher.

Suddenly, he heard a very soft voice say, "Hello."

Joey sat up and looked around, but he couldn't see anyone. So, he laid back down by the stream only to hear the voice again.

The voice sounded bubbly and a little like running water. Joey didn't know where it was coming from.

Now, you need to understand that Joey knew the forest like the back of his hand. He had played in it, walked in it, sat in it, and had seen it in every season. He had even named some of the trees that he thought had faces. He knew the forest well, and he had never been lost in it.

He knew where the stream was deep enough to swim before it reached the pond. He knew where to find tadpoles and to see the baby fish, and where the best places to fish were. But in all the times he had been in the forest, he had never heard this voice.

He began to search for the source of the voice. He didn't see or hear anyone. People or kids often made a lot of noise walking in the forest. Joey soon discovered that when he moved away from the stream the voice became softer or disappeared. When he moved closer to the stream he could hear it softly murmuring, "Hello, hellooo, hello." But he still couldn't discover who it was that was speaking.

Joey went back to the stream and sat down. He closed his eyes and waited. Yes, there it was again. It was louder now and more insistent.

"Hello!"

Joey opened his eyes. He had read many books about fairies and elves. His parents said they weren't real, but he still kind of believed in them. He looked around again wondering if he would find an elf or fairy who might be talking to him. But he couldn't see one. He was very puzzled and a little bit disappointed. He closed his eyes again.

This time the voice said, all bubbly and watery, "I am here. You are sitting right next to me!"

Joey was sitting next to the stream. It took him a minute to figure out who was speaking. Finally, he asked in wonder, "Water, are you the one who is talking to me?"

The water was so happy that Joey could finally hear it talking.

"Yes, yes, it is me! I have been trying to talk to you for such a long time," it bubbled. "It is so hard to speak with humans. Most water, water from all over the world, said people couldn't hear us, but I have done it! I've done it!" It sounded almost like the water was laughing. "I am so happy you can hear me. We have so much to discuss," said Water. "I have so much to tell you!"

Joey was shocked. Was he going crazy? Was he hearing voices? Was the water in the stream really talking to him? What did Water mean when it had said the other water in the world didn't think it was possible to speak with humans? How was his stream in contact with all the other water in the world?

He pinched himself. *Ow!* That hurt, so he knew he wasn't dreaming. He still didn't know what to think. He knew if he told others he could hear water talking they would laugh at him or think he was crazy. He couldn't believe it himself. He sat by the stream quietly. He kept thinking to himself, *Wow! Is this really happening?*

Water was quiet for a bit before it said, "I want to tell you about you and me and how we are connected. I'm part of you and you are part of me. I am part of the trees, the plants, and the rocks. I am part of everything!"

Joey thought that didn't make any sense. How was water part of him, and he part of the water! That was very strange. He sat there and thought about it.

After a minute Water spoke again. "Where to start? Where do I start my story? I know what I want to say to you, but I am so excited that I don't know where to begin. First, I am a sentient being. Do you know what that means?"

Joey was about to answer when he heard his mother and father calling him. They sounded a bit anxious. He looked around and noticed that the sun was setting, and it was getting dark. He hadn't realized just how long he had been in the forest.

He yelled to his parents, "I'm coming!"

Joey said to Water, "I'm sorry, but I have to go."

Water replied, "Come back soon because we have so much to talk about."

Joey promised he would be back, but he wasn't sure what to do. Nothing like this had ever happened before. He was interested in talking to the water, but he was also a bit afraid.

Chapter 2
In Trouble Again

As Joey walked out of the forest, he could see his mother was upset.

His mom asked, "Where have you been? We have been calling and calling you! You know you are not allowed in the forest on your own!" She sounded close to tears and Joey knew that was because she had been scared.

Joey said, "It is okay, Mom. I was down sitting by the stream, and I didn't realize it was so late. I really think I should be allowed to go there on my own. I am ten years old!"

His mother replied, "I don't care how old you are, you are not to go there on your own."

It was now Joey's turn to be close to tears since the forest was his special place. He pleaded, desperately, "I must go there. It is quiet and I can think there."

His mother started to say no yet again, but his father interrupted her.

"I think it may be time to reconsider the rules, but not right now," he said. "Let's go inside and have dinner. After we calm down, we can discuss what would be reasonable."

After dinner, his father said, "Let's talk about what rules would be fair now that you are ten years old."

Joey's mother said, "I don't like Joey going into the forest by himself. He could get hurt."

Joey's father replied, "I think going into the forest by himself is safe. But he may not swim alone. Joey, you must always have me or your mom with you to swim."

Joey suspected his father knew he had been sneaking into the forest on his own.

Joey asked, "What about fishing?"

Joey's father and mother both exclaimed, "No fishing on your own. It is too easy to lose your footing and fall in!"

Joey reluctantly agreed. He knew the stream was deeper where he fished, so he did understand his parents' concerns.

His brother and sister had been listening quietly to the discussion about Joey's visits to the forest, especially his older brother.

His brother asked, "But I can swim on my own, right?"

Again, both parents said, "No. You may only fish with a buddy and no swimming without an adult."

That seemed fair to Joey, so he said, "Well, I have homework to finish."

"Off you go then," said his mother. "And don't give us a fright like that again."

Joey went to get his backpack and his homework. He sat down at the kitchen table to do his work, but he couldn't concentrate. He kept thinking about the water speaking to him. He didn't know what to believe! Should he tell his parents? Finally, he decided that he needed to know more before he told anyone else about what happened today. He was noticeably quiet, and his parents could see he was not doing his homework.

His mother asked him, "What are you dreaming about?"

Joey replied, "I'm not dreaming. I am thinking."

"Oh," said his mother. "Well, stop thinking and finish your homework. It is almost bedtime."

She was concerned that he might be getting sick because he was so quiet, but she didn't say anything else. After going to bed, Joey lay thinking about the water talking to him for a long time before he finally fell asleep.

Chapter 3
What to Think

Joey didn't know what to do. Should he go back to the stream or should he stay away? He loved the stream and didn't want to stay away from it, or from the forest. But he couldn't believe he had heard water talk! He wished there was someone he could tell.

His family was very normal. Both his parents worked and were very busy. His older brother was always out with his friends or playing music. His sister had her own friends and belonged to several clubs. She always stayed after school. Sometimes, his siblings let him tag along but not often. Anyway, it was more fun to be with his own friends.

His siblings, and probably his parents, would just laugh at him if he told them he had heard water talk. They would say it was just his imagination. But there was one person who he felt would understand. Everyone thought she was a bit strange and might even be a witch. Her name was Alice and she lived down the road in a pretty, but a very ramshackle house.

In the summer, her house was covered by so many climbing roses that you could hardly see it. She grew all sorts of fruits and vegetables. She often gave Joey's family some of her delicious tomatoes, berries, and other vegetables. Still, she was strange, and he was slightly afraid of her. She talked to her plants!

Wait, did that mean she could hear them? Joey thought to himself. After all, the water had spoken to him.

Joey decided he couldn't tell anyone yet. Water hadn't told him anything yet. He would wait and see if it had been real or if he had just imagined the water talking to him. He didn't think he had dreamed it, but he would go back tomorrow to see if it happened again.

But Joey had soccer practice the next day, so he couldn't go back to the stream. The day after, it was karate, and it was too late to go into the woods when he got home. On Thursday, his friend Eva came over. She was a very good soccer player, and he liked her a lot, but she didn't like being in the forest. She said it felt creepy and she preferred to play soccer.

And then on the weekend it rained. Not a gentle rain. It really poured. His mother said they hadn't had so much rain in a long time. And his father told Joey not to go into the forest without him, because the stream might have jumped its banks. His dad wanted to go with him to make sure it was safe. Joey was so frustrated!

It was Sunday evening when it finally stopped raining. He and his dad went into the forest, and it was super wet. There were pools of water everywhere. And sure enough, the stream had jumped its banks. It looked like a torrent because it was running so fast. Joey had never seen the stream like that.

His father said, "Just as I thought. The stream is too dangerous right now to visit. We'll have to wait a few days and see what happens. I am so happy that our house is up on the hill. Otherwise, we would have had water inside the house!"

Joey was extremely disappointed. However, he could see that the place he usually sat was underwater. He hoped the moss would be okay.

Chapter 4
Back in the Forest

An entire week had passed before Joey visited the stream. He rushed home from school to go into the forest. Luckily, his father was home early from work so he could go with Joey. His dad wanted to check that the stream had calmed down. It was still wet in the woods, but the stream looked more like its old self. So, his father said Joey could stay, and he set off for home.

Joey sat by the stream for a long time, but all was quiet. He didn't hear anything and concluded hearing the water talk had been his imagination. He was about to leave when he heard the voice.

"Took you long enough!"

Joey replied, "Well . . . I came as soon as I could. I wasn't allowed to come earlier because of all the rain, and the fact that you jumped your banks!"

Water sounded proud as it exclaimed, "Did you see me? Wasn't I incredible? I was running so fantastically fast and there was so much of me that I managed to jump over my banks! It was so much fun. But I guess I was a bit too wild for you. I wouldn't have been able to talk to you had you come earlier as I was too busy. I was having so much fun and couldn't stop."

Joey simply nodded, still a bit confused by the fact that water was talking to him.

Water suddenly remembered their prior visit and questioned, "What was I saying when you left so abruptly? Oh yes, I was telling you that I was alive and sentient. I was going to explain to you that everything is alive. Everything is connected: you, me, the trees, the plants, the soil, and the rocks. Everything! Do you know how much of you is made up of me?"

Joey asked, "What do you mean?" He felt so confused and didn't understand what Water was talking about.

Water replied, "Your body is more than 60 per cent water. So, I make up more than half of your body. You and I are connected because I am part of you."

"Really?" asked Joey. He knew there was liquid in his body. He drank water when he was thirsty, but was it really true that more than half of him was water?

Water told him, "You can check my facts if you like. Ask your parents or your teacher. Or you can go to the library."

Joey remembered that he had learned something about this at school, but he couldn't remember the details. Still, Joey was surprised that Water knew about schools or libraries.

"And there is more to know," Water said. "You can live without food for about one or two months, but without water you can only live for about three days!"

Joey was amazed. "Really!" he said. It was the only thing he could think to say.

Water continued to share. "I react to feelings, you know."

Joey hadn't known this and almost said "Really" again, but he stopped himself.

Water explained that it felt great, just like Joey did, when others loved it or were happy and grateful to have it. It felt bad when it sensed hate, anger, or sadness.

Water told Joey, "You can check that out too. There was a human called Masaru Emoto and he did a lot of experiments with me. He took very pure water like me and placed it into very small vials and put labels on them like 'love' or 'hate.' He spoke words to the vials that represented the emotions. Then, he froze the vials. After the water had frozen, he cut small slivers off the ice (ice is what I become when I am frozen). He was very surprised to find that kind words like 'love' or 'happy' made me form beautiful snowflakes when I was frozen. But nasty words made me just become a blob. I didn't form any snowflakes."

Joey frowned a little, picturing Water as a frozen blob.

Water continued, "The same result happens with music. If he played classical music or upbeat, pleasant music like the Beatles, the water would form beautiful snowflakes. But if he played hard rock or loud, harsh, and disjointed music, the water froze into a blob."

Joey was quiet as he listened. He didn't know what to think or say. First, he still couldn't get over the fact that Water was talking to him. And, if what Water was telling him was true, it was amazing! If it was true, could the way you feel impact the water in your body?

"You can go and check it out if you don't believe me," Water said sadly, because it felt that Joey didn't believe what he was hearing. "Check out Masaru Emoto's work in the library."

Joey nodded as he thought about what Water was telling him.

"There is so much more I can tell you," Water exclaimed. "I can be in four different states. I can be a liquid, as you see me now. Or I can be solid, like when I am ice. And I can be steam, which you see when the kettle or pot is boiling. Recently, your scientists found a fourth state. Let's not worry about that last state right now."

Joey felt like his head was spinning because of all the information Water was giving him. He knew that they had learned some of this in school, but he had never thought about water like he was right now. Water had always been just water, ice was just ice, and steam was steam. He realized now that water, ice, and steam were all different states.

He was feeling a bit overwhelmed and wanted to go home and think. He also thought that maybe he should check out Water's facts too!

So, Joey told Water, "I have to go now." He politely said goodbye. He still felt kind of silly talking out loud to Water, but he did it anyway.

Water said, "Sorry you must go. I have only just started to tell you all about me. But goodbye. Come back soon and we will continue to chat."

Joey went home and he was very quiet as he thought about everything Water had told him. His mother even asked him if he was feeling okay because he was so quiet. He told her he was fine, but she still touched his forehead to see if he had a fever.

Chapter 5
Checking the Facts

The next day was Saturday so Joey looked up on the computer how long a person could last without food and water. He found that Water was correct. He could hardly believe it. But he didn't really want to go back to the forest just yet. He needed a chance to think some more.

Luckily, his mother wanted him to go shopping with her and later his father wanted to go for a hike. Joey was too busy to think much about what Water had told him.

Sunday was also a busy day. His grandparents came for a visit, and he had to help with some chores at home as well.

The next day was Monday. Joey went to school and couldn't wait for recess. During recess, he went to the library on his own. He had never been to the library without his class before and wasn't quite sure where to start.

The librarian was called Miss Sunshine by all the kids. It wasn't her real name, but she was so friendly and happy that everyone called her by that nickname. She asked Joey if she could help him find a book. He told her that he wanted a book about water and he thought the author was called Masaru Emoto. He told her he didn't know how to spell the author's name.

The librarian said, "I know exactly who you are talking about, and I love that book! Kids don't usually ask for it, but the pictures in it are so beautiful. Let me get it for you."

Miss Sunshine went off and soon returned with a big book that had a blue cover. She put it on the desk and asked Joey, "Who told you about Mr. Emoto? Are you doing a project about him?"

Joey didn't know how to answer her question. "No, I'm not doing a project. I am just interested in water."

The librarian replied, "Well, look through this book and I can give you a smaller book written by the same author called *The Hidden Messages in Water* that you can take out with your library card."

Joey began to look through Mr. Emoto's big book. The photographs were amazing. He could hardly believe the pictures were of water. Under each picture, it said the name on the label for each bottle of water. It was just like Water had told him. Joey was so excited. The pictures showed the frozen water was just a blob for the mean words. And the frozen water with words like love and joy was so beautiful.

Joey kept turning the pages, looking at the pictures, and reading the captions until the bell rang, signalling the end of recess. He could have sat there all day looking at the pictures. He asked Miss Sunshine for the little book she had promised him so he could take it home.

He went back to class in a daze but he was so excited. It was hard for him to concentrate in class, and he was glad when it was time for gym. He ran around and managed to forget about Water as he played basketball.

Finally, school ended, and he went home. As he took his lunch box out of his backpack, the water book fell out. He started to look at the book. There was a lot of writing in the book, but in the middle, there were more pictures. Again, he was amazed by the beauty of the snowflakes. He realized that Water was teaching him some important things.

If I get really angry, maybe the water in my body does change and if I get really happy, it will change again! he thought to himself.

Joey began to think more about what Water had told him. What would happen to the water in a person's body if they got angry or if someone called them a mean name? He decided that he would ask Water about that. He was excited about the book and showed it to his mother while she was making dinner.

She said, "Very nice, dear."

Joey could tell she was too busy to really think about the book and what amazing things it was saying about water.

His homework took him a long time because he kept stopping to look at the book. He wondered what else Water would tell him, but it was too late to go into the woods to visit the stream. He vowed he'd go the next day to visit.

But Joey had forgotten that the next day was soccer and the day after was karate. So, it would be another three days before he could visit with Water again.

Chapter 6
Back to the Stream

Finally, Joey found time to go into the forest to visit with Water.

As he was sitting down beside the stream, Water said, "It is about time! I've been waiting for you."

Joey nodded and said, "The water book is so beautiful! I can't stop looking at it."

"Oh," said Water. "You did some research. Excellent! Excellent! But there is much more I must tell you. Make yourself comfortable. It is going to take a long time!"

Joey settled himself on the soft moss. He took off his sandals and put his feet into the water.

"I have a question for you Water. What happens to the water in my body if I get angry at someone or if someone gets angry with me?"

"A very good question," said Water. "In either case, the water in your body gets upset and causes you to not feel very well.

You feel sad, or maybe you will cry. Crying is good because it puts good endorphins into your body, and you will start to feel better. They help the water in your body to recover."

"What are endorphins?" asked Joey.

"They are chemicals produced in your body that make you feel good. There are so many ways you can make them. By laughing, or by exercising. Joggers feel great after they run. You can make yourself and the water in your body feel better by moving your body. You can walk, swim, or do similar activities."

"Now to continue our chat. Where did I stop? Oh yes, I remember. Did you know if there was no water on the earth, it would be a desert, like the planet Mars? You wouldn't be able to survive without water. All living things need water. If trees don't have water, they can't grow. Did you know that trees are more than 50 per cent water? It is the same for plants, animals, and people. They all need water to live."

Joey looked around. The trees looked solid to him. The plants didn't look watery, and his body didn't feel watery. He remembered Water telling him that he was 60 per cent water. But he didn't tell Water he was a bit confused.

Water continued, "Water covers 71 per cent of the earth. And one drop of water is connected to every other drop of water on the planet. Everything is connected. I said it before, but it cannot be said too many times."

Joey asked, "But how can that be? Your stream is connected to the lake, but not to the ocean."

Water began to explain to Joey how all water was connected.

"Your scientists call it the Water Cycle. It is an endless process that connects all water together. It joins the oceans, land, and atmosphere together."

"How does it join them together?" Joey asked.

"Well, water becomes vapour when it reaches the right temperature, which is when it becomes really hot. The water vapour rises into the sky and becomes a cloud. That is called condensing. When it rains or snows, water is returned to the ground. And you saw how powerful I can be when there is a storm," bragged Water.

Joey said, "Wow! That's cool. I've never thought about it like that before." Joey thought about how he had always taken water for granted. It was just always there. You turn the tap on, and water comes out.

But Joey understood enough about the importance of water that he would get upset when he heard about people polluting water and the earth. It made him angry when he walked in the forest and saw garbage that had been left behind. He often would bring a bag to collect any trash he found during his visits so he could keep his forest clean. His grandmother had taught him to do this since she always brought a trash bag along whenever they would go on a walk together. Even when they went to the beach! She always picked up the junk left by others. Her motto was, "If we don't do it, who will?"

Water could sense that Joey was getting tired, so it asked, "Is that enough for today?"

"No," said Joey "I want to hear more."

"You clean stuff with water, right? You even clean *yourself* with water, and that makes me dirty."

"Right," Joey said, rather hesitantly. He wasn't sure what Water was going to tell him. He was afraid Water would tell him to stop using it.

"How do you think I get clean again?" asked Water.

Joey didn't know. He had never thought about it.

"Your scientists have found ways to clean me with sand and micro-organisms. They have built water treatment plants to keep me clean. They can remove the dirt and toxins that humans put into water. There are many plants like irises and water lilies, and fungi (mushrooms are one type) that can be used to clean water. The plants clean the water because they eat the toxins, which helps them to grow."

Joey was surprised that plants could be used to clean water. Then, he had a funny thought. He imagined a dandelion standing at a sink while it washed Water just like his parents did when they washed the dishes. He started to laugh.

Water thought Joey was laughing at it and said, "Hmmph!" Water stopped talking.

Joey said, "Oh, I wasn't laughing at you. I was picturing a dandelion standing at the sink, washing you. It was a funny picture."

Water said "Hmmph!" again, followed by, "Well, that is all for today."

Joey said goodbye and ran home. It was a good thing that they had finished talking. Joey could hear his mother calling him in for supper.

As he ran out of the woods, she said, "Finally! I think I am going to get a gong and bang it when supper is ready."

Joey thought that was a great idea. He thought it would be so much fun to bang a gong or even a drum.

"What about using my drum?" he asked.

His mother just laughed as they went in for supper.

Chapter 7
More Voices in the Forest

The next day Joey had a play date with his friend Zach. Zach loved playing video games, but they decided they would spend half of the afternoon playing in the forest. Not that Joey's mother would allow them to play video games all afternoon anyway!

They went quite deep into the woods where it was gloomy and a bit scary. They imagined they could see bears and really scared each other by yelling out "Bear!" or "Snake!" Then they would run and climb a tree or hide.

They were hiding behind a huge tree that had fallen, crouched on the ground, when Joey heard a little voice.

"Get off me!! You are squishing me!" the voice cried out.

Joey turned white with fear and whispered to Zach, "Did you hear that?"

"Hear what?" Zach replied.

"I thought I heard a voice," Joey whispered back, still a bit scared.

Zach said in a loud voice, "No!" But he was now a little scared too, so he said, "Let's go back and play video games."

Joey said, "Sure, but let's walk back on the path so we can see what is under our feet."

They were walking back to the house when Joey heard the voice again.

This time it said, "Whew! What big oafs!"

Joey turned around to see who had spoken, but he couldn't see anything.

Joey wondered if he should tell Zach about his talks with Water. But he decided not to because he didn't want to be teased. Zach wouldn't believe him anyway. But he would tell Water about the voice deep in the forest the next time they talked. Could it be a fairy or an elf that had spoken? Joey reminded himself that he didn't believe in them anymore. Well, not all that much anyway.

Joey used to think he could see fairies and elves. No one else saw them, even when he pointed them out. So he began to believe he was just imagining them and after a while he stopped seeing them too. That had been when he was much younger and now, well, he knew better. But wait! If he could hear the water talk, then maybe he really could hear the fairies and elves too!

Chapter 8
The Role of Trees

Once again, it was a few days before Joey could return to talk with Water. There was a different reason every day that made it too late for him to go into the forest and sit by the stream.

Joey's parents were worried about how much time he was spending alone in the forest. No matter how much he told them he liked to be alone and loved to be in the forest, they still felt he should be with his friends. So, they started to set up play dates for him when he wasn't at karate or at soccer. And he did like to play soccer and he loved karate. But he liked to be alone too. Sometimes he didn't want to go play with the other kids, but his mother always said he had to!

Finally, on Saturday morning he had some free time. His mother wanted him to go shopping with her, but he hated going with her to the store. In the end she said he could go into the forest and she made him a sandwich to take with him. He was so happy.

When Joey sat down by the stream Water didn't talk to him. Joey was worried that Water had missed him and thought that Joey wasn't coming back. Maybe Water was angry.

"I'm sorry, Water. I couldn't get back here until now," he said. Joey told Water about his parents wanting him to be with his friends more. Before he could finish speaking Water spoke.

"Oh, okay! I thought you had lost interest in learning about me."

Joey said, "Oh no. I love to hear what you are telling me. I am learning so much!"

Water said, "Well, today I am going to talk about the trees. I know a lot about the world because I am part of everything and, as I told you before, I travel all over the world in the form of clouds and rain. There is water in everything, even in the rocks, but that is a story for another day. I get to see so many different places on the earth," Water bragged. "There are underground streams, lakes, and even seas!" Water was very excited to share his knowledge with Joey.

"What was I saying? Oh yes, the trees," Water answered itself. "As I told you before, trees are half water."

Joey shook his head in confusion. "They look so solid," he said.

"Well, looks can be deceiving," Water said. "If you weigh 'green' wood, it will be about half water and half carbon. And trees are the reason there is enough oxygen to breathe and support life. Have you heard about photosynthesis?"

Joey nodded. He remembered learning about it at school.

"Well," said Water, "how it works is that trees and plants take water from the soil, light from the sun, and carbon dioxide from the air, and turn them into food for themselves and into oxygen. Then, they put the oxygen back into the air."

Joey remembered the poster at school showing the process.

"This is good for you" continued Water, "because too much carbon dioxide is bad for humans. It is called a pollutant! And the oxygen that is released is important because you need it to breathe!"

Joey took a deep breath.

"Did you know that in the spring the tree uses water to move sugar from its roots to the rest of the tree? The sugar water is called 'sap.' People tap maple trees to collect the sap and boil it to make maple syrup."

Joey nodded again. He liked maple syrup on his pancakes.

"See? You did know that trees contain water," Water said. "But that wasn't what I wanted to talk to you about. I do get distracted sometimes. I wanted to tell you about the life of a tree. They are alive, you know."

Joey did know that. He had seen dead trees in the forest. He and his father often went to look for dead trees to use as firewood. They looked for trees that were dry. If they were still wet, they didn't burn as well.

Water continued to explain about the life of the tree. "Trees can be as big below the ground as they are above it. And there are mother trees in the forests—these are the oldest trees. They have the most connections with the other trees. Trees communicate with each other and look after the young trees by sending them nutrients through their roots."

Joey found it all very interesting. Who knew older trees looked after the younger trees. Just like people!

"They even take care of sick trees by sending them substances like medicine to help them get stronger. Trees behave just like other species, such as humans and animals. In fact, they act the way all humans should behave."

Joey had never heard people being called a species before. But he knew it was true, even if it was not familiar. And if everything was connected, then humans were just one of many species!

"It also means that humans have to stop cutting down so many trees, especially the really big, old ones!" Water exclaimed. "There is a human scientist called Suzanne Simard who wrote a book for grown-ups that explains all about the mother trees.

"Trees also provide homes for the birds," Joey said.

"Yes, and for lots of other animals and bugs. And when trees die, they provide the soil with the nutrients it needs," said Water.

Joey asked, "How do they communicate? Do they have their own language that we can't hear?"

"Yes, they do. They send messages to each other through the air or the mycelium."

"Mycelium?" Joey asked. "What is that?"

Water explained, "It is a huge organism made up of very, very small fibres or filaments of fungus. The fungus grows underground, and it connects all the roots of the trees together. Its flower is a mushroom. Do you like to eat mushrooms?"

Joey hesitated before he said, "Sometimes, but I do like to go hunting for them. I'm learning which ones you can eat, and which ones are poisonous."

"That is good," said Water. "You need to know which ones are safe to eat. You can't eat every mushroom!"

Water continued to talk. "The mycelium forms a mat under the soil and connects all of the tree roots. Some humans call the root mycelium connections the 'wood-wide web.' It stretches for miles and miles all over the earth. Every time you take a step, you are walking on it. A man called Paul Stamets knows lots about mushrooms, mycelium, and trees."

Joey knew he would be going back to the library to do more research!

"The trees provide sugar to the mycelium and the mycelium provides nutrients and carries their messages. It is a good arrangement."

Joey thought so too. "Wow! Trees clean the air for us, create oxygen, store carbon dioxide, provide fruit and nuts for people, look after each other, and create places for animals, birds, and bugs to live. They are very busy!"

"They are," agreed Water. "They even warn other trees if a bug or an animal like a giraffe starts to eat them. The other trees will start to produce a substance that the giraffes or bugs don't like, and that will make them stop eating those trees. Trees are a model of cooperation, generosity, and altruism. That means they think about others before themselves."

Water had explained what altruism meant before Joey could even ask!

Water then spoke in a voice that Joey felt was very stern. "It is very important to think about that. Trees heal living creatures, including humans, by releasing substances that contain lots of healing ingredients like natural antibiotics. That is why spending time in nature helps people to stay healthy, puts them in a good mood, and can even help to heal them."

Joey was amazed.

"Trees help to regulate the atmosphere and stabilize the climate. Diana Beresford-Kroeger wrote a great book called

To Speak for the Trees. She wrote about how trees do this. It is a grown-up's book, but you could read about her on the internet or listen to a video."

"I like to watch videos on YouTube," Joey said.

"She said if everyone planted one tree a year for the next six years that humans could help stop climate change."

Joey thought that sounded like a good plan.

"Trees can even play music," said Water.

"What? Do you mean when they creak in the wind at night, or when the wind rustles their leaves?" Joey asked.

"No," replied Water. "There are some people who live in a place called Damanhur that have invented machines to record the sounds trees make and then translate the sounds into music. They have even played music in the forest and the trees have played along with them!"

Joey wasn't sure he believed that. He felt that was something he needed to check out. He wished he had brought a notebook to write down some of this information. He hoped he could remember everything that Water had said so he could look it up at the library later.

Water stopped talking and they sat quietly together for a long time. Joey ate his lunch as he thought about everything Water had told him today.

Then, he decided it was time to go home. He had meant to stay longer, but there was so much to think about. Plus he wanted to write everything down before he forgot it. And he was very tired from learning so much.

"I am going to go now," Joey told Water.

Water stayed quiet, so Joey got up, said a polite goodbye, and walked home, deep in thought.

Chapter 9
Someone to Talk To

When Joey got home, he began to write down everything he had learned from Water into his biology binder from school. He chose this binder because both trees and water are studied in biology. He did his best to spell the difficult words by sounding them out. He wished he had someone to talk with about everything he was learning. He felt he might burst if he didn't talk about it. It was all so strange. But who could he talk to that wouldn't laugh or tease him? Who would believe him that he was talking with Water?

He went through everyone he knew once again. He couldn't talk to anyone in his family, that was for sure. He considered telling his friend Eva but the only thing she thought about was soccer. Plus, she would think he was crazy and would tell everybody about it. Next, he thought about Zach, but Zach didn't really like being in the woods and preferred playing video games. So, he probably wouldn't understand.

Joey was stumped. Maybe he could talk to the librarian. Miss Sunshine was very helpful. She might understand, but she might tell his teacher and then who knows what could happen!

Joey had one aunt who might understand. But Aunt Melody lived far away. She was his mother's sister, and much more open-minded than his mother. He didn't see her very often, only in the summer when she came to visit. He liked her because she was gentle and kind.

Aunt Melody did something called Reiki. He wasn't sure how it worked, but it was about using energy through her hands to heal people. He thought about it some more and decided he couldn't just pick up the phone and tell her that he could talk with water.

Joey thought again about his neighbour, Alice. He had never been to her house alone before. He always went with his mother to visit or to take her cookies. He didn't have anything to take to her and he felt anxious about going to visit on his own. But he decided he would go and see her. She was always in her garden, so she must know a lot about plants. He knew she even talked to them! He felt she would be the best person to talk with about his conversation with Water.

Chapter 10

Joey Visits Alice

Joey decided it was best to go see Alice before he lost his courage. So, he got up, walked out of the house, down the driveway, along the sidewalk, and all the way to her gate. His heart was pounding in his chest, and he wanted to run back home, but he thought, *Now or never!* He had hoped she would be working in the front garden so he could just chat to her over the fence. But she was nowhere to be seen. Joey pushed open the gate. It creaked so loudly it scared him and made him think of witches and scary movies. He nearly ran home, but it was too late to escape.

Alice appeared from around the corner of the house. She looked surprised to see him but gave him a welcoming smile.

"I always know when someone comes into my yard because of the gate. That is why I don't oil it. How are you, Joey? Is there something I can do for you?"

Joey didn't know how to begin, so he just said, "I wanted to talk to you." He suddenly felt shy.

Alice said, "Come on around to the back. I have some lemonade and we can have a chat." She didn't know what a young boy like Joey would have to talk to her about, but she was willing to listen. Joey knew in that instant that she was really nice!

Alice went inside the house through a side door. After a while she brought out the lemonade and two glasses, and they sat down at the table on her patio.

Joey was quiet, but finally he said, "This is going to sound really weird . . ."

Alice encouraged him by saying, "I love weird."

Joey went on, feeling a little better. "One day when I was in the woods by the stream, I heard a voice . . .," and the whole story tumbled out.

Alice listened silently, and when he finished she said, "Wow! What a wonderful thing to have happen to you! I would love it if Water would talk to me!"

Joey just sat and looked at her. He really hadn't expected that reaction. It made him happy and relieved to have found someone to talk with. Someone who was open to believing him.

Alice continued, "What important things you have learned about the water in our bodies! It really is important to try not to stay angry or upset, so the water in our bodies can remain like sparkling snowflakes." She paused and asked wistfully, "Can I come with you one day? I have been reading about how water has a memory, and I would really like to talk to Water about that. Do you think Water would talk to me?"

Joey didn't know. He didn't want to spoil the friendship he was building with Water. He thought for a while. *It sure is nice to have someone to talk to, who understands and isn't laughing about what I am saying. But what if Water only wants to talk to me? But Alice is so excited about this, and I bet Water would like her.* Joey thought it over some more before he replied.

"Yes, I think that would be okay. Let's see if Water will talk to both of us." He paused, then continued, "But I think I should ask Water first if I can bring you."

Alice said, "That is a great idea! Let me know what Water says. If it doesn't want to speak to me, you can always ask it my questions for me. When will you go back to visit?"

Joey said, "Well, I could go back now. My mom and dad are out but they know I spend a lot of time in the woods."

"Do you now?" Alice asked. "I guess you have met the wood sprites and fairies then."

Joey looked at Alice in disbelief. His eyes grew big, and he exclaimed, "I didn't know grown-ups believed in fairies. I don't know if I've met them, but when Zach and I were in the woods I thought I heard a cry and someone say, 'get off me!' But I couldn't see anyone or anything. It spooked me. Zach said he didn't hear anything, but he wanted to get out of the woods really quickly."

Alice didn't say anything, and just drank her lemonade. Joey finished his drink and decided it was time for him to leave.

"Well, I'll be off then. I'll come back after I have talked it over with Water and let you know if I can bring you along."

Joey thanked Alice for the lemonade and ran off. He felt lighter and didn't feel as anxious now. It wasn't all just up to him anymore and he had a friend to confide in! He really hoped Water would be okay with Alice coming to visit. He also hoped that if she came Water would still want to talk to him.

He didn't go straight to the stream. Instead, he went home and made himself a snack so he could have a picnic beside the stream. He packed an apple and a bag of chips. He was thinking about what else to take when his older brother Mark came into the kitchen.

"What are you doing?" Mark asked.

"Making myself a snack for a picnic," said Joey.

"What do you have so far?" Mark questioned him.

Joey showed him what he had packed for his picnic.

Mark said, "I'll make you a great sandwich if you share those chips with me."

Joey agreed and Mark made him a fantastic sandwich with cheese, lettuce, and tomato. He cut the sandwich and the apple in half and gave them to Joey. Joey wrapped them up and poured half of the chips into a bowl for Mark.

"Where are you going?" asked Mark.

"I'm going into the woods and down to the stream," said Joey.

"What is so fun in the woods that you spend so much time there?" asked Mark.

"I just like it in there," answered Joey. He wasn't going to tell Mark about Water. His brother would just laugh at him and tease him about it. Mark didn't have much of an imagination. He would never understand how Joey and Water were friends.

Chapter 11
Back to the Stream

So, off Joey ran to go meet Water. Mark watched him go and thought to himself that Joey was a strange kid.

Joey arrived at the steam out of breath. He sat down and started to eat his snack while he waited for Water to speak. A squirrel came closer to investigate and sat near him, watching Joey carefully. Joey tossed it a piece of the bread. Water hadn't spoken yet, so Joey started the conversation.

Joey said to Water, "You can share my snack too if you like."

"That is very generous, but I don't need to eat," answered Water.

Joey hesitated but began to tell Water about his talk with Alice.

"I'm not sure you will like this, but I had to tell someone about us chatting together. I thought and thought, and finally came up with someone who wouldn't laugh at me or tease me. Her name is Alice, and she lives near our house. I told her all about our conversations and she really listened. She would like to come and meet you. She has lots of things she wants to talk to you about. Would it be all right if I brought her to meet you?"

Water said, "I know Alice. She often comes to sit beside me and put her feet into me. She is very calm and I think the fairies like her. I guess it would be all right if you brought her, but not every time. We don't want to get too distracted as I have a lot to teach you."

Joey was relieved that Water didn't want him to bring Alice every time he came to visit. His friendship with Water would be safe. But he was stunned to hear Water talk about the fairies too. Maybe they were real!

Joey continued to eat his snack, sharing it with the squirrel and a robin who also joined them. They all sat quietly for a while doing nothing except enjoying the peaceful day.

Then Water said, "Where were we?" It seemed to ask that a lot!

Joey said, "You were telling me about the trees and the my-my-my . . ., something related to mushrooms. I can't remember the word."

"Oh yes, I remember," said Water. "The word is mycelium. It is very important. It is all over the world and forms huge mats to help the trees and plants to communicate with each other. It helps them to grow and to keep the forest healthy. It is so tightly packed that one of your scientists, Paul Stamets calculated that there is so much of it under the ground that we step on three hundred miles of mycelium with every step we take.

"Wow! That is a lot," said Joey.

"Humans are just discovering it again. They knew about it a long time ago. Now they are rediscovering they can use it to make things like clothes and houses. And mycelium can clean the water! And some mycelia have chemical properties that can help save the bees and stop them from dying off! It can do so many important things!"

Water was excited and was talking very quickly. It was hard for Joey to keep up.

"There are people very far away, in central Europe, who still remember the old ways and they make hats out of mycelium."

Joey thought a hat made out of mycelium sounded kind of funny.

"Humans knew a long time ago that everything was connected. They also knew that plants and animals communicate with each other. But people forgot about this and started to pollute me and the earth. Some still remember, but only a very few," said Water sadly.

Joey agreed it was very sad.

"People think they can pour and dump harmful stuff into me, and I can take it out into the ocean so it will disappear. But it doesn't disappear. It pollutes the water, and it harms or poisons the fish and everything else that lives in the water and near the water. Everything is connected."

Joey thought it was all very complicated. He didn't like to hear about people polluting the water and the earth. He knew there was pollution because he had heard the grown-ups talking about it. He hated when his parents talked about global warming because it was scary. Yet, people still did things they shouldn't. If grown-ups knew what was causing it, why didn't they stop?

Joey didn't know what to say. Water sounded so sad. He thought maybe he should go and get Alice. Perhaps she could say something to make Water feel better. But Joey stayed sitting next to Water, saying nothing, and feeling sad with Water.

Finally, Water said, "You are a good listener. Sometimes it helps just to be listened to and feel that a human understands, even if he can't do anything to help right away."

Joey heard his mother calling him and looked around. He felt like he was waking up after a dream. He didn't know how long he had been sitting by the stream. It was time to go home.

"Goodbye Water. I'll bring Alice next time."

Water called out, "Goodbye, see you soon."

Joey went home, but he was thinking about so many things. Humans were polluting the water! You could make houses out of mycelium! Everything is connected! There was so much that needed to be done to change the world, but where did he start?

He really wasn't hungry, but he knew by the setting sun that it must be dinnertime. It wasn't long ago that he had eaten his snack.

As he sat down at the table, Joey told his mom that he wasn't very hungry. He could tell that she was worried he wasn't feeling well again. But his brother, Mark, was there and answered for him.

Mark said, "I made him a sandwich at five o' clock."

Joey's Mom was irritated about Joey eating that late. "Why did you do that? You knew I would be making dinner soon."

Mark didn't answer. He just shrugged his shoulders.

His mother rolled her eyes and said, "Well at least I know he isn't sick!"

They all laughed together.

Chapter 12
Saving the Forest

During dinner, Joey's brother, sister, and parents talked about a petition they had signed to protect the forest behind the house. Some developers were wanting to cut down part of it to make room for more houses. They wanted to use the lumber from the trees to build houses. Joey listened carefully to what they were discussing.

Joey asked, "Why don't they use the mycelium to build houses? Then they would not have to cut down any of the trees."

His siblings and parents stopped talking and looked at him.

"What did you say?" asked his father.

"I said mycelium," replied Joey. "I just learned about it. It grows everywhere under the earth and mushrooms are its flowers."

"Never heard of it," said his brother. "I am going to google it."

He picked up his phone and a few minutes later exclaimed, "He's right!"

His father said, "All the more reason for us to protect the forest."

Joey remained quiet, but he was thinking about what Water had said. About how people needed to be planting more trees, not cutting them down.

The family discussed some of the things they could do to stop the forest from being cut down. They talked about making flyers and delivering them in the neighbourhood.

Joey said, "I can help deliver the flyers."

His mother added, "We are trying to get a big group together to try to change the developers' minds. To show them that people don't want to lose the forest."

Joey said, "Great, I'll come!"

His mother was delighted he wanted to come. She was thinking it would mean he wouldn't always be in the forest sitting alone. Even though Joey assured her he liked to be alone sometimes, she still worried.

The next few days were a blur for Joey. He was busy with school, soccer, karate, and delivering the flyers. He met a lot of people who also wanted to help save the forest.

His parents were happy. They had a great turnout at the rally and a good meeting with the city and the developers. People even came from outside the area to support them. No one wanted the trees to be cut down or the forest destroyed. His parents wrote a petition to make the forest a protected area. Joey was excited. He had so much to tell Water!

Chapter 13
Alice Meets Water

It was the start of the third week since Joey had last seen Water before he could find the time to go into the forest again. He slipped over to Alice's house first to tell her that Water would like to meet her. She was ecstatic! He had seen her at the rally and when she had helped to deliver the flyers, but he hadn't been able to tell her that Water had agreed to meet her.

Alice grabbed her water bottle and hat, and they went off into the forest together. Joey was glad no one had seen them because he could imagine all the questions about why he was with Alice. Not that it was wrong, but how would he explain it to others? He couldn't tell them about Water.

As they made their way down to the stream, Joey instructed, "You have to sit quietly for a bit until Water greets us, and then I will introduce you."

Alice said, "Okay." But she could hardly contain her excitement. She was so happy to finally have a chance to ask all her questions. She said, "I hope I will be able to understand what Water is saying!"

Joey said, "You just have to remember that everything is connected: you, me, the trees, the water, the grass, the moss, and even the stones."

"Did Water tell you that?" asked Alice.

"Yes," said Joey.

Alice replied, "I think about it this way. Everything is connected because everything is energy, including water."

Joey didn't say anything in response because he was thinking about what she had said. Reaching the stream, they both sat down. Alice and Joey waited very quietly beside the stream.

Eventually, Joey said, "Hello, Water." There was no answer for a long time.

Finally, Water answered. "Hello, Joey! Welcome, Alice!"

Alice smiled so broadly that Joey thought her face would crack. She had so many wrinkles, but she was beautiful when she was happy. Then she began to cry.

"I am so happy I can hear you. I was so worried that I wouldn't be able to. I was afraid that only Joey could hear you," she said between sobs and then she laughed with joy.

Joey thought to himself, *Oh dear, what is going on! She is laughing and crying at the same time.* He was concerned because grown-ups normally didn't do that.

Alice looked over at Joey and said, "Don't worry, Joey, I am just fine. I feel like this is a dream come true. I've always wanted to communicate with other species, but I am not very good at it. I communicate with my plants with the help of my pendulum."

Joey asked, "What is a pendulum?"

Alice showed him her pendulum. It looked like a piece of wood on a chain. She held it between her fingers by the chain.

"When I suspend it like this, it will swing back and forth. I have programmed it, so that it will answer the questions I ask with a 'yes,' or 'no.' I could show you how to use it sometime or you could google 'Letter to Robin' and learn how to do it yourself," Alice said.

Joey nodded, interested in learning more about it.

She continued, "Even though I talk to my plants all the time, I only 'hear' them when I use the pendulum. I ask them questions through the pendulum and get answers from them. Things like if they need to be watered or need some mulch. I don't actually hear them, but the pendulum shows me their answer. But this is different. I heard Water welcome me inside my head!"

Joey was puzzled. He felt he had conversations with Water just like he did with everyone else. Oh well, it must be something to do with being a grown-up.

He began to tell Water why he hadn't been to visit for so long. He told Water that he had delivered flyers to help save the forest from the developers' plans to cut it down and to turn the space into homes. Joey felt that Water knew about the plan already, but he still wanted to talk about it with Water.

Then Alice said, "I hear you have been teaching Joey about water, the trees, and the mushrooms. I have so much I want to teach him too. But I feel that I still have so much to learn."

Water knew that was a big admission for a human to make. It thought that most humans think they know everything, but most don't know very much. Water didn't comment but was pleased with Alice's comment.

Water asked Alice, "Do you have any questions for me?"

"Oh yes," said Alice. "I have been reading about water having a memory. Is that true?"

Water replied, "Of course I have a memory. I remember you because you sometimes put your feet into the water. You are 60 percent water. Everything has its own energy and I remember them all. I share my knowledge with the rest of the water. Everything is connected, you know."

Alice paused. "Yes," she said, rather haltingly. "I do know that everything is energy and that everything is vibrating all the time," she added. "And I think that the way it works is that everything is connected through that energy—right?"

Water was a bit miffed. "Well, I like to think it is all connected because of me. Water is in everything, you know. But I suppose it could be because everything is energy," he conceded. "Of course," he said, "your scientists are finding out that energy and matter are one and the same."

Joey had only heard the word "matter" when his mother asked him, *what was the matter*. He didn't think that was what Water meant.

So, Joey asked, "What is matter?"

Water replied, "It is things—plants, trees, you, me, and everything you can see."

Joey thought *oh no, something else to try to understand.*

All three of them sat in silence for a bit.

Joey thought about how he liked it better when it was just him and Water. He was a bit upset that he had brought Alice because he didn't like to share Water with anyone else. But she was so happy! And then he reminded himself that he didn't have to bring her every time he visited Water.

Water must have been feeling the same thing because suddenly it spoke to Alice.

"You know, you can talk to me from anywhere, Alice. It doesn't just have to be here, for I am everywhere."

Alice thought that Water was probably correct, but she liked it by the stream.

She said, "I know that, but it is so peaceful and green here. I like it here. I can really relax, which helps me to communicate. Would you mind if I visited you on my own?"

"Not at all! Come anytime. I am always here," joked Water while extending the invitation.

Alice said that she had to go home, and Joey was glad. He was very happy that he had someone he could talk with about Water. But he was also pleased to have some time alone with Water. Plus, he could avoid any potential questions, since they wouldn't be leaving the forest at the same time.

Joey said, "I'm going to stay for a while," as he lay down on the moss beside the stream.

Alice said goodbye to Water and to Joey and then said to Joey, "Thank you for bringing me." Then, she headed off home.

After Alice had left, Water spoke again. "Such a nice human. At this rate I will have to reconsider what I think about humans. I now have met two that I like."

Chapter 14
Everything is Energy

Joey was surprised that Water had only met two humans that it liked. It had been all around the world after all.

Joey said, "I think you would be surprised at how many people want to save the forest and are working to do that. You would probably like them too."

"Maybe," said Water, sounding like it was thinking about it, but then it changed the subject. "Since Alice spoke about energy, I think that is the next thing we must talk about. As she said, everything is energy. Not the type of energy that makes you get up in the morning, but what you and everything around you is made of. You look solid but, you're really made up of very tiny particles that are always vibrating. Even what you call air is made up of those same particles!"

Joey thought, *what is Water talking about?*

"Usually, you can't see the energy with your eyes, but it is there," said Water. "The particles are so small and are vibrating so fast that they are hard to see, but some people can see the energy surrounding living things. It is called an 'aura' and is the energy field that surrounds people, plants, trees, and even mountains. The aura has beautiful colours if a person or a plant is healthy but it is rather dull if they aren't."

"Did you know that you can focus your energy and use it to do things?"

"What do you mean by focus?" asked Joey.

"Focus means to concentrate. So, if you concentrate very hard you can use energy to clean water. You can send healing energy to someone who isn't well. Or you can put healing energy into water and give it to a sick person to drink. The energy will help them feel better."

Joey thought about this. "Grown-ups can do that," he said.

Water replied, "No, anyone can do it. You don't have to be grown-up. But you must learn to concentrate on what you want to happen. You can't have all sorts of other thoughts in your head when doing it. You can only think 'I am cleaning the water.' Have you ever heard of meditation?"

Joey replied, "Yes, we do it at school. You sit like this."

He demonstrated the lotus position, sitting cross-legged with his back straight.

"Well," said Water, "it is also how you learn to clear your mind so that you can concentrate and send the energy anywhere you want it to go. Humans have done many experiments about this process. You can look them up."

"Oh boy! Now I have even more to research," Joey groaned.

But truthfully, Joey was very happy. He felt so optimistic. He could help to save forests, like he did with the petition and the rally. And now he was learning that he could clean water and even heal people. Wait! Could he heal animals and plants too?

Water must have read his mind because he answered Joey's unspoken question.

Water said, "You can heal animals and plants too. You can heal anything once you put your mind to it."

"Wow!" said Joey. But he decided he would do the research first before he started to tell people about what he had just learned.

Maybe that is what Reiki is all about, he thought to himself. *I will have to ask Aunt Melody when she comes to visit in August.*

Joey was so grateful to be able to talk with Water. He had so many more questions, but he was sleepy, so he lay down on the soft moss next to his friend Water.

He fell asleep and had a dream. In his dream he could see beings made of air and who were made of so many beautiful colours. And the colours were all around the trees and plants too.

Suddenly, he woke up. He could hear his mother calling him.

"Water, I have to go, but I had such an amazing dream."

"Remember it and we can talk about it the next time."

Joey said, "Bye," and ran off, heading home.

When he reached his home, he was panting from running so far. But he was still thinking about his dream. Was it a dream or a daydream? Had he actually fallen asleep? He thought he should write his dream down, so he didn't forget it.

Later when the family was eating dinner Joey told them about his ideas to help make a difference.

Joey said, "You know, we need to plant more trees, and not just cut them down. I wish there was a place where I could get lots of kids together to plant trees and make a new forest. Then I would really be helping to stop climate change."

"That would help," said his father, "but I don't know of any empty land around here. And people wouldn't like it if you just started planting trees all over. But, it is a good idea. Let me think about it some more."

After dinner, Joey began to write about his dream. He wondered if he had seen some fairies. He would talk to Alice and Water about it.

He announced, "I'm going over to Alice's house."

His mother asked, "Whatever for?" She was surprised because she didn't know that Joey was now friends with Alice.

Joey had to think fast. Going over to Alice's house had just slipped out, but he wasn't ready to tell his mother about Water yet.

So, he said, "I met her when we were handing out the flyers to save the forest. She told me I could come over any time I wanted to help her in her garden."

His mother shrugged. "I didn't know you were interested in gardening. But I guess it is better than going into the woods and being alone for hours."

Joey didn't agree because he loved the forest. And he wasn't alone; he was visiting with Water.

Chapter 15

Nature Spirits in the Garden

Joey headed out to visit Alice. He wanted to tell her about his dream and to ask her what she thought about it. The gate creaked loudly but this time Joey wasn't scared. Again, Alice appeared from around the side of the house.

"Hi Joey," she said. "Want some lemonade?"

"Sure," said Joey. Alice's lemonade tasted so good. She used real lemons to make it.

They headed around to the side of the house and Joey continued into the garden. Alice went into the house to get the lemonade. Joey took the time to look around. The garden was amazing. It was filled with flowers of every colour and size and in between were rows of all sorts of vegetables and fruit. There were tomatoes, cucumbers, beans, and kale. Joey didn't like kale, but even it looked good in the garden surrounded by the raspberries and blueberries. There were even apple and pear trees. He was full of awe.

Alice came out with the lemonade, and they sat down in the garden.

Joey said, "Your garden is so beautiful!"

And then he noticed the label on the jug. It said 'Love.'

He said, "Do you know about the experiments with water and feelings?"

Alice replied, "Yes, I do! That is why I have labelled my jug!" Joey was impressed.

Alice told him she was glad he liked her garden and then asked, "So, do you have something new to tell me?"

Joey exclaimed, "Oh, yes!"

He told her all about his dream and asked her if that was what the fairies looked like.

Alice smiled broadly. "Yes. Most people can't see them. But that doesn't mean they aren't there. I call them nature spirits."

Joey said, "They are like energy."

"Exactly!"

Alice continued to share more, "There are two places in the world that I know of where humans have been working with the nature spirits for a very long time. They have been growing spectacular vegetables and fruit for years. One is Findhorn in Scotland, and the other is Perelandra in the United States."

Joey looked around the garden as he thought about spirits living there.

"I am trying to do that in my garden with my pendulum. Although I can't see or hear the nature spirits, I know they are here. I ask them questions about the soil, how much to water, and where to plant so that the plants will thrive. And you can see the results."

Alice looked around her garden with pride.

Joey said, "Yes, I think this is the most beautiful garden I have ever seen."

Joey told Alice about his idea to get kids to help plant trees. Like the author Diana Beresford-Kroeger had said, if everyone planted one tree every year for six years in a row, they could help stop climate change. He told her his dad was thinking about a place where they could plant trees.

Alice said, "What if each child planted their first tree in their own garden?"

Joey thought that was a great idea. But how could he earn money to buy some trees? Suddenly, he was imagining a worldwide movement of kids planting trees. He told Alice what he was thinking about.

Alice said she would also think about how to raise some money for the trees and where they might plant them. But she agreed it was a good plan and said that he might become famous one day. Joey became shy at the thought and said he had to go. He didn't want to be famous. He just wanted to help save the forest and nature. And to help kids like himself to make a difference. It was important that he did something because everything is connected. He wanted to make a difference.

Joey went home and started to write about his ideas. He would go to the stream again on another day to talk it over with his friend Water.

He asked his siblings what he could do to raise some money. His brother suggested a lemonade stand. Joey thought it was a good idea but wondered how much he could earn because their street was so quiet. His sister suggested he move it to a corner where there was more traffic. She even offered to bake some cookies for him to sell.

Then his sister said, "Joey, that won't bring in much money and it will take a lot of time. Why don't you write something about what you want to do, and we could post it on the internet to raise money through crowdfunding."

"What is crowdfunding?" Joey asked.

"That is when you have a great idea and let people know about it through the internet and ask them to donate money so you can use it for your project," answered his bother.

Joey thought that was a great idea. He was really happy when his sister and brother agreed to help him.

The next day Joey went into the forest and down to the stream to visit with Water. He was brimming with excitement. He wanted to tell Water all about his ideas and about raising money to buy some trees. Water knew about crowdfunding, and thought it was a great idea.

Water said, "That will be a wonderful way to start to change things."

Water reminded Joey again that everything is connected. Joey felt that he understood that now. He said "I think the first step is to get kids involved and thinking about protecting and cleaning up the environment. These are some of the ways they can really help. And when my father finds us a place, the kids and I can all plant trees. Water agreed!

About the Author

Ellen Lewinberg has had several careers in her life. She began work as a social worker in South Africa and did further training in England, earning a master's degree at the London School of Economics and Political Science. After moving to Canada, she studied to become a psychoanalyst, and treated both children and adults in private practice for more than twenty-five years.

Following a health crisis in 2002, Ellen slowed down a little and changed her focus. She opened a flower shop and learned Reiki and healing bioenergy. She has had a bioenergy healing practice for the past fifteen years. Ellen's passions are reading, gardening, water, trees, and walking in nature.

Ellen decided to write a book for children and their parents, to introduce the ideas that she accepts daily as part of her working with energy. These are concepts that much of society is only just beginning to think about. She believes it is vital for our future to accept and understand the connectedness of everything.

Acknowledgements

I would like to give a big thank you to my husband John Torry for his support, editing, and general help while I wrote this book. I also want to thank my daughter Tanya and her wife, Jina for their enthusiasm, and my grandchildren, Eli, Martin, and Isaac for all their comments and suggestions.

References

I have provided my referenced resources and encourage you to investigate if you wish to learn more.

Books

Beresford-Kroeger, Diana. *To Speak for the Trees: My Life's Journey from Ancient Celtic Wisdom to a Healing Vision of the Forest.* Random House Canada, 2019.

Emoto, Masaru. *The Hidden Messages in Water.* Simon and Schuster, 2001.

Grace, Raymon. *The Future Is Yours: Do Something About It!* Hampton Roads Publishing, 2003

Pollak, Gerald H. *The Fourth Phase of Water: Beyond Solid, Liquid, Vapor.* Ebner & Sons, 2013

Simard, Suzanne. *Finding the Mother Tree: Discovering the Wisdom of the Forest.* Allen Lane, 2021.

Stamets, Paul. *Mycelium Running: How Mushrooms Can Help Save the World*. Ten Speed Press, 2005.

Online Resources

Beresford-Kroeger, Diana. YouTube, September 28, 2020

Center for Nature Research — Perelandra Ltd.: https://www.perelandra-ltd.com/

Findhorn Foundation: https://www.findhorn.org/

Grace, Raymon. Dowsing https://www.raymongrace.us/about-dowsing.html#/

Letter to Robin. https://lettertorobin.wordpress.com/

The Music of The Plants - Damanhur Foundation: https://www.damanhur.foundation/project/the-music-of-the-plants/

Manufactured by Amazon.ca
Bolton, ON